The Purple Cow Mystery

by Elspeth Campbell Murphy

Illustrated by Nancy Munger

Timothy   Sarah-Jane   Titus

Do not lie to each other.

Colossians 3:9a

BETHANY BACKYARD®

MINNEAPOLIS, MN 55438

The Purple Cow Mystery
Copyright © 2002
Elspeth Campbell Murphy

Cover and story illustrations by Nancy Munger
Cover design by Jennifer Parker

YOUNG COUSINS MYSTERIES is a trademark of Elspeth Campbell Murphy.

Scripture quotation is from the HOLY BIBLE, NEW INTERNATIONAL VERSION®. Copyright © 1973, 1978, 1984 by International Bible Society. Used by permission of Zondervan Publishing House. All rights reserved. The "NIV" and "New International Version" trademarks are registered in the United States Patent and Trademark Office by International Bible Society. Use of either trademark requires the permission of International Bible Society.

The poem "The Purple Cow," quoted on pages 7 and 27, was written by Gelett Burgess (1866–1951).

Published by Bethany House Publishers
a Ministry of Bethany Fellowship International
11400 Hampshire Avenue South
Bloomington, MN 55438
www.bethanyhouse.com

Printed in China.

Library of Congress Cataloging-in-Publication Data

Murphy, Elspeth Campbell.
  The purple cow mystery / by Elspeth Campbell Murphy.
    p. cm. — (Young cousins mysteries; 5)
Summary: Upon finding a mysterious note demanding a secret cookie recipe in exchange for a kidnapped purple cow, Sarah-Jane and her cousins devise a plan so that they can see this rare bovine.
  ISBN 0-7642-2498-0 (alk. paper)
  [1. Cousins—Fiction. 2. Cookies—Fiction. 3. Mystery and detective stories.] I. Title.
  PZ7.M9516 Pu 2002
  [Fic]—dc21
                                        2002006083

Contents

Chapter One
The Windy Day

"'I never saw a purple cow,'"
Sarah-Jane said to her cousins.

Timothy and Titus stared at her.

"Okaaay..." said Titus.

Sarah-Jane was always coming out
with strange little things like that.

They didn't make sense
until she explained them.

"It's a poem," said Sarah-Jane.

"Okaaay..." said Timothy.

Sarah-Jane was always reading poems
and learning them by heart.

"It's a poem about a purple cow," said Sarah-Jane.

"There's no such thing as a purple cow," said Timothy.

"I know," said Sarah-Jane. "That's what the poem is about."

"There's a poem about something that doesn't exist?" asked Titus.

"Right," said Sarah-Jane. "It's called 'The Purple Cow.' Do you want to hear it?"

Timothy and Titus sighed.

"Do we have a choice?" asked Titus.

"Not really," said Sarah-Jane.

"OK. Let's hear it," said Timothy. Sarah-Jane smiled.

"'I never saw a Purple Cow,
    I never hope to see one,
    But I can tell you, anyhow,
    I'd rather see than be one!'"

"Interesting," said Titus.
"But why would you want to be
any kind of cow?"

Sarah-Jane groaned.

"I'd like to *see* a purple cow, though,"
said Timothy. "Wouldn't you?"

"Sure," said Titus.

"AURGGH!" cried Sarah-Jane.
"There *is* no purple cow!
You will never get to see one!
I'm sorry I brought it up!"

Just then a gust of wind
blew a sheet of paper onto the porch.
It was a note.
Sarah-Jane read it aloud.

Chapter Two
The Mysterious Note

The cousins read the note again.

And again.

"Okaaay..." said Titus.
"Now *that's* weird!"

Timothy said, "Why does it say,
'see your purple cow *again*'?
We never saw a purple cow
in the first place!"

Sarah-Jane said, "And why does it say,
'your grandmother's
secret sugar cookie recipe'?
Does Grandma even *make* sugar cookies?"

The cousins thought about this
for a minute.

"Maybe it doesn't mean
our grandmother," said Sarah-Jane.

"Huh?" said Timothy and Titus.

Sarah-Jane said,
"Maybe the note is for someone else.
And it just blew here by mistake."

"There's no name on it," said Titus.

"And there's no handwriting,"
said Timothy. "The words are cut out."

Suddenly Sarah-Jane said,
"This is a ransom note!
This cow has been kidnapped!"

Timothy and Titus stared at her.

"How do you kidnap a cow?"
they asked.

Sarah-Jane shrugged.

Then she said slowly, "You know…
If we go to the library
at three o'clock,
we might get to see it."

"See what?" asked Timothy and Titus.

"The purple cow," said Sarah-Jane.

"S-J!" said Timothy and Titus.
"There's no such thing
as a purple cow!"

"I know that!" said Sarah-Jane.
"I'm just saying what the note says."

The cousins read the note again.

Titus said, "The kidnappers
won't give the cow back
unless they get the secret recipe."

Timothy said,
"So if we want to see the cow,
we have to leave them
a secret recipe for sugar cookies."

Sarah-Jane said,
"There's no such thing
as a purple cow, you know."

"We know," said Timothy and Titus.

Chapter Three
The Secret Recipe

Sarah-Jane said, "We don't have somebody's grandmother's secret sugar cookie recipe."

"We know," said Timothy and Titus.

"So what can we put on the rock?" asked Sarah-Jane.

The cousins thought about this.

"Does it have to be *the* recipe?" asked Titus. "Couldn't it just be any old sugar cookie recipe? I mean, would the kidnappers know the difference?"

The cousins thought about this.

Timothy said, "One time my mother got a good recipe for oatmeal cookies from a box of oatmeal."

"Interesting," said Titus. "So maybe a box of sugar would have a recipe for sugar cookies."

They checked.

And they were in luck.

It did.

At first they tried
to copy the recipe by hand.

"That won't work,"
sighed Sarah-Jane.
"It looks like a kid did it."

"A kid *did* do it," said Titus.

"The computer?" suggested Timothy.

"The computer!"

agreed Sarah-Jane and Titus.

Timothy and Titus

read the recipe out loud.

Sarah-Jane did the typing.

They checked it over carefully.

Then they printed it out.

They had to agree it looked

pretty good.

"There!" said Sarah-Jane.
"Now all we have to do
is go to the library
and leave the recipe
on the big rock."

"There's not going to be
a purple cow. . . ." said Timothy.

"No, of course not. . . ." said Titus.

"I know that. . . ." said Sarah-Jane.

Chapter Four
The Big Rock

At the library,
the cousins put the recipe
on the big rock.

Since it was a windy day,
they put a little rock
on top of the recipe
to keep the paper from blowing away.

Then they scrunched down
behind the big rock.

They settled down
to see what would happen.

They didn't have long to wait.

Sarah-Jane looked at her watch.

The big hand was on twelve.

The little hand was on two.

Two o'clock.

The cousins peeked out to see
who would come along.

To their surprise,
they saw two nice-looking old ladies
coming toward the big rock.

The ladies did not have
a purple cow.

But one of the ladies carried
a bumpy tote bag.

"Look!" cried one of the ladies.
"It's Grandmother's secret recipe!"

"Our plan worked!" cried the other.

The cousins looked at one another.
Maybe their own plan
hadn't turned out quite right. . . .

The cousins crawled out
from behind the big rock.
It took a while to explain
what they were doing there.

"We're sorry," said Sarah-Jane.
"It's just that—
we never saw a purple cow."
The ladies smiled.
One of them said,

"'I never saw a Purple Cow,
   I never hope to see one,
   But I can tell you, anyhow,
   I'd rather see than be one!'"

The other lady said,
"That was one of our favorite poems
when we were little girls."
And then she opened the tote bag.

Chapter Five
The Purple Cow

"A cookie jar!" cried Sarah-Jane.

"That's right," said one of the ladies.
"Our sister collects them.
This is her latest one.
She bought it at an antiques store.
It's quite valuable."

"And you kidnapped it?" asked Titus.

The ladies looked embarrassed.

The second one said,
"It was a silly plan, we admit.
But our sister makes the *best*
sugar cookies you ever tasted!"

"Yes!" said the first lady.
"She says she found
our grandmother's secret recipe
in the attic.
We didn't even know there *was*
a secret recipe.
And now our sister won't share it."

"So we kidnapped her cow,"
said the second sister.
"But I guess we'd better take it back."

The cousins agreed
that this would be a good thing to do.

They went along to see
what would happen.

"Look at this," cried the third sister.
"Someone stole my pretty purple cow!"

"Uh—not exactly," said her sisters.
"We kidnapped it to make you share
Grandmother's secret cookie recipe."

"Um . . ." said the third sister.
"I don't really have a secret recipe."

"WHAT??" cried everyone together.

"No," said the third sister. "I'm sorry!
I wanted to feel special.
So I made up that story about
finding a recipe in the attic."

"Then where *did* you get the recipe?"
asked Sarah-Jane.

"From the back of the sugar box. . . .
Why are you all laughing?"

The End